p o e t r y
ˈpəʊɪtri

noun

a collection of words to help join together a planet of people longing to feel connected. An expression of feelings to help people feel listened to and loved.

acknowledgements

Mum
I wouldn't be who I am without you, I am moulding around you and our lives are now entwining. We are existing together, but not because we have to, because we want to. I came from you, you made me, you gave me life and helped me grow it, and what a beautiful garden we are creating, together.

Grandma
You gave me so many seeds to plant. It wasn't until I was older and ready to do so, but I held onto them for all this time. You might not be here to see them grow, but you have shown me so many different colours, vast beauty, gentleness and courage. Maybe now you are the sun looking down on me, so the growth may continue. Together again.

Grandad
A man of few words but so much stability and guidance. Very much like an oak tree, somewhere to sit and clear your mind, somewhere to relax and worries to fade away. A simple life, not much was needed but everything was enjoyed. I will look for you in Nature. With mum and I planting, Nan glowing, and you standing tall, who could want anything else from a garden. Together always.

— a beautiful garden

I have decided to sit with myself
to let the feelings pass over me
everything that needs to be felt
reflecting and understanding
to not run away from my brain
and in time, we might become friends
so pull out an extra chair
whilst we find the beauty in it all
the impact in the stillness
the fight in the gentleness
the silence in the loudness
the sureness in the uncertainty
I am sitting with myself to find answers
and this is where we begin

the recipe for reading this

servings

one book to last you forever

time

as long as you need to heal

ingredients

an open mind
one cup of tea, or coffee
two spoonfuls of sugar
one pen
one piece of paper, *to write your feelings too*
a handful of courage
a splash of hope — that things will be ok
trust in yourself
a whole packet of biscuits
empathy — but most importantly
love, so much love

directions

create a calm space for yourself, somewhere that you feel safe. Dim the light just enough so you can read the words, put some gentle music on in the background, maybe something without too many words, open this book and let yourself feel everything that you need to, *don't be embarrassed, this is a safe space, you are all welcome here.*

contents

impact in the stillness
silence in the loudness
fight in the gentleness
sureness in the uncertainty

impact in the stillness

the little things sit amongst us
modest and gentle
they teach us to slow down
they give us meaning

a quiet life

I know why I feel alone
I don't think I am an old soul in a young body
a hard stone in a juicy peach
I am a simple soul in a complicated body
a lightbulb in a moroccan lamp
try to catch the colour if you can
it will change with each room I am in
because not one room feels like home
I belong somewhere quiet
a candlelit flame
for the nights we don't sleep
and when we wonder what time it is
we look to the sun

the butterfly effect

it's a quiet morning in August, the sun is rising and the birds are calling, your tea is brewing in your favourite mug. You're not sure what to do with your day, let alone your life, but you are alive, you are present in this moment, and you are feeling, *never stop feeling*. You are seeing beauty in the stillness, calmness in the breeze as it wraps itself around you, you close your eyes with a feeling of nostalgia, it's almost as if you're a child again, you hold the simplicity in your little hands, and let it go like a butterfly, hoping the same wind will take it away, and one day it may find its way back.

Then before you know it, it's a quiet morning in September, and a butterfly has just landed on your shoulder.

and I sink my teeth into poetry because it's my only form of escape, and I tell myself not to get lost in these words, *just understand them*, and I bite down hard because it's the only time my jaw relaxes, and I let my mouth speak "this too shall pass" in the mirror whilst holding onto my words, because I'm scared if I let them go, I will have to bump into them one day, *and on this day* — I will have to tell them why I didn't listen

little red van

I saw this little red van on a hill
oak panels hugged the outside
a tree crafted into a home
it is what Mother Nature would've wanted
I have had many conversations with her
about my need to live independently
my need to start fresh
where the air is so clear I am breathless
run away in a little red van and not look back
she said it's something I must figure out myself
she gives us the elements to build our home
but we must be the ones to drive it
this little red van had a steel chimney
inside a pile of birch from another tree
the warmth of freedom
to use the land we have been given
is priceless
the less you have, the less you need
the richer you will be
just a red van and some trees
and endless memories

if I could live this life again
I would come back as myself every single time

better together

if it wasn't for the flowers I don't know if I'd be here
I nestled into the petals like a loved ones shoulder
I needed to know how to survive the rain
how they grow through it
the pollen looked like Christmas snow
I held it out for the bees
they knew I meant no harm
there is no sixth sense in nature
just instinct
I like it that way
no need to overthink when the sun looks after you
when the rain feeds you
the most dangerous part a human hand
if I was too beautiful I would be taken
so I put store into protection
together we are untouchable
a sunflower field, me and my sisters
lifting each other
growing together

the world is waiting for you, what are you waiting for?

you will fly

I sat and made origami
I thought if I understood that
I could understand myself
shapeshifting bodies
folding under fingertips
I knew I needed stronger material
it is something I can work on
I built some paper planes
to watch them fly
catch the air under their wings
like a bird of prey
but I am not the target today
I close my eyes and soar the skies
I can go anywhere
bending under pressure
sodden with downpour
parts of me starting to unravel
changing directions
but I remember that
a difficult journey
is still a journey

back to my roots

I am lost in the trees
pulling on the weeds
I am climbing higher, until I get grazed knees

I am stumbling on the ground
I am both lost and found
I am dizzy from all the spinning around

I am swimming in deep water
still trying to be the best daughter
loving with all that her mother taught her

It is confusing being out in the wild
yet I used to love it, hiding as a child
so maybe being lost, will be ok for a little while

I want to dance in the dandelions
I want them to tickle my toes
on a summer evening in june
I want to laugh again

I love watching them grow   *I love watching you grow*

they taught me in silence

things haven't always felt easy
the growth of bone to more bone
and fat to more fat
planted in the soil but needing a solitary pot
just so I don't compare my growth to others
to not always being picked by gentle hands
and not always being placed in the sun
ripped from the root after finally sitting with myself
and becoming neighbours with the slender sunflowers
the only thing that felt easy
was the love of the sun
the one feeling to not be suffocated by
an orange glow shrouding my stalks
she met me with kindness
somewhere soft - where the best fruit grows
the big juicy strawberries that don't care for size
always picked by curious hands at flooded markets
the pebbles of rain skimming my petals
I didn't need to feel the ripples
only watch the journey
four bounces across the open stretch of water
to sink and rest on the seabed
only to be found years later by longing hands
time didn't matter and neither did size
we age and grow and fall and rise
we wilt and die and corrode and survive
but ease has only come through observation
I've never been told, only shown
all those years planted in one place
I was never bored, never alone

I haven't seen much light lately
but still I'm waiting patiently by the window

a sweet life

I will be happy one day
I am a good person
I will feel love in abundance and relish in its glory
I will do somersaults in the grass and let my inner child take over
I'm not sure if this is an affirmation list or a poem
and I'm not sure if I believe in anything anymore, manifesting or wishing
but I think as long as I am a good person — *kind, happy*
with a heart as pure as the water
from the mountains, I am climbing
and it's a long way to the top, *I am patient*
I think life will treat me well, well enough
a sweet dessert, that I never want to stop eating
and whoever said life is like a box of chocolates
never had just one left, and enjoyed every single bite

love isn't always a walk in the park
but true love, *is just walking in the park*

sunday morning

I want to eat pancakes with you in the morning
finish them whilst we're still yawning
feel like nothing else is important
but the weight we're both supporting

Listen to Loyle Carner on vinyl
finish each line like it's a recital
Sun of Jean, the sun is vital
showing us her every cycle

I don't need a home because you are mine
I am confined to your every line
those four walls in which you designed
always keep me intertwined

The world is moving fast for me
but you slow me down and that's all that I need
you grounded me with the roots of your tree
and together we flourished, steadily

new beginnings

I was born in april
so I guess you could call me a spring baby
I was birthed when the trees changed colour
I grew up with the shooting flowers
effortless and gentle
I celebrated with the baby lambs
we were naive and innocent
dependent
I followed the crowd
hatched out of an egg
to open my eyes to see my kin
flying above me
but I couldn't fly yet
only follow
just born and already waiting for my resurrection
to grow inside a tulip
the easter flower
a spring baby waiting to bloom
after all of these years
a spring baby waiting to fly

I promise, you will be loved
full and unwavering
you will be seen
honest and quiet
you will be touched
soft and purposeful
you will be loved, *I promise*

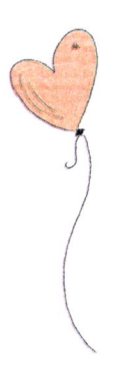

trust yourself

I don't believe in manifestation
and I don't want to see another self help book
what do you suppose we give to the girl who can't see past today
fifty pages of wishing? *when she needs a gentle touch*
there is no way other than up the grassy hill
but you have to reach places nobody has been before
culminated by the light you find within yourself
it isn't inside a guide, the guide is inside you
the reflection, the overwhelming head to heads
it has to be felt in real time, in the present
and one day you will have come so far
you won't even remember the taste, *the smell*
and sometimes the wind will blow
and you will be reminded of the courage
and they will say to you
I wish I had your strength
and you will say
you don't need to wish — it is already inside you

girlhood

I am craving friends who want to chase the sun
girlhood is running to the light at 5am
we are cold but we feel alive
and just when the strawberry skies blend into burnt orange
making us morning breakfast — a soulful smoothie
we realise
nothing matters when we have each other
there is a bond between women that binds us tightly
maybe we're keeping eachother warm without even knowing
a glow that can never be replicated
the sun is rising and we are together
what a perfect time to be twenty five

I found love

I found love in my coffee mug
a big handle so I didn't burn my fingers
I made sure to put milk in before the water
this way I didn't burn the coffee
it's probably the most important thing I've learnt today

I found love in buying fresh flowers for my table
so I know that I need to keep something else alive
I've struggled with doing that recently
but it feels good to watch something grow
a feeling of belonging
and it's nice to know I'm needed
it's probably the most exciting thing I've done this week

I found love in lavender baths
it's the most vulnerable I can let myself be
I let the water kiss my skin
I can be alone with my body for a while
I've been trying to list all the things I love about her
maybe I will try writing it on the steamed glass
it's probably the hardest thing I will do this year

I found love in peace
for so long it haunted me
I couldn't let myself think
I didn't want to, but we stopped fighting
me and my brain
I let the thoughts come and go, like waves hitting the stones
they only hold substance when I let them
it's probably the most important thing I've learnt in this life

nostalgia

often in the bird calls is when it hits me
or when the sun is so peaceful
and a breeze wraps itself around strangers
walking, talking, laughing
observing human connection and craving ours
when the sun is so constant
a day where worries just burn away
and everything feels alright for just a second
those are the days I wish you were here

the pin of sunlight

I never quite fitted in
so I was left to squeeze into places I didn't belong
I shrunk to become something, and I bent to adjust myself
then before I knew it, I forgot who I was
I lost parts of me by giving them away
and I never asked for them back
because maybe they need them more
so, crooked and half empty
I wiggled out of these tight spaces towards the pin of sunlight
I patched myself up with the dirt I was learning to walk upon
for the first time I could feel my feet
before I knew it
flowers started to grow in the places I was lonely
the pin of sunlight turned into a tunnel
I could fit into it perfectly
this feels like home

living for contentment not validation
finding joy in the quiet hours
existing gently in preparation
to grow into my confident flowers

there is always enough time in the day to love yourself
even when the sun is setting under the big tree
— *there is still time*

she's like the wind

it's funny how most of my life has been governed by the wind
my mum used to say
"if you pull that face, the wind can make it stay like that"
so I sat under the trees with a grin as big as the sun
hoping mother nature would burn it onto my skin
a constant imprint — so that when I didn't feel as safe
I could look in the mirror, and be reminded of the person I wish to be
now at twenty five, blowing out never ending candles
they tell me, *you change like the wind*
and it's hard with anxiety, because not one thought is stable
one day I am a ginger leaf being spun in circles
the next - I am an olive leaf whistling like a comforting tune
but like the wind, I am both everything and nothing
invisible and impactful
modest and fierce

silence in the loudness

waiting in the water

I unintentionally isolated myself from people
as a cry for help
a destructive trait I recognise
floating solo in a big pond
cries echoing off of quiet shores
I wonder if they heard me
they definitely noticed my absence
but they still didn't come to my rescue, nonetheless
I don't blame them, how were they to know
cries and laughter can look similar in the dark

how brave it is to love
in a world as harsh as this
and if that's my only measure of success
then I've got nothing left to miss

and some days I listened to Gregory Alan Isakov and
felt like I was in a film, and other days Hozier made me
believe in love again, and times I got lost in Loyle
Carners words, and I wondered if this is where I belong,
somewhere more meaningful, or was it nice to just escape
— every once in a while

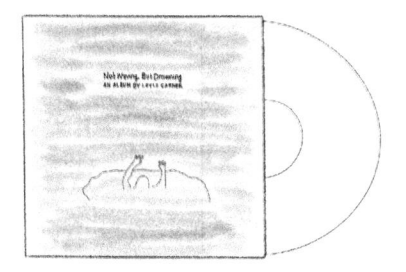

the weight of living
is sitting heavy on me today
she sat on my lap
I let her in
maybe if I carried her on my back
together our journey could begin

the weight of living

the weight of living
is slowing me down
but maybe that's what I need
because sometimes going fast
isn't all it seems to be

to use weathered as an insult
denies the beauty of the sun
the softness of the rain
the courage of the wind

looking out for you

I think losing grandparents isn't talked about enough
and I think what we don't talk about is their love
as they raise us like their own
not always in our family home
but a second one, where we're always welcome
and the memories of nostalgia
that's where we first felt them
but they never seem to stay long enough
to see the person they helped grow
and when it's time to show them
we need some time to borrow
I'm walking gently looking for signs
the confidence in the sun when it shines
and I'm wrapping myself around the memories
which are strong enough to carry me
but sometimes it's your arms that I need
before the sun finally goes to sleep

growth isn't always beautiful, *said the flowers*
sometimes you need to hide before you can shine, *said the sun*
there is comfort in the darkness but you can't stay there, *said the moon*
I can't always be your safe space, *said your home*
it is wonderful to feel free, *said the wild animals*
there is so much waiting for you, *said the earth*

The versions of you that have existed, have left imprints on people that you don't even realise. You are still preserved in memories, so older versions of you never really disappear. You are still someone's first love, first kiss, first heartbreak, *and you always will be*. You leave little pieces of you everywhere you go, so whenever you feel alone, just know that you exist in so many places that you don't see. You will continue to do this as you evolve, so as long as you lead with love and kindness, you will be remembered that way for always, no matter what version of you that is. Sixteen or fifty, there are pieces of you everywhere.

love language

it was how I loved you that said so much about me
an open line of communication, I drew it with ease
I followed it in the hopes that you'd meet me halfway
a safe space inside my home, somewhere to lay
I waited on the blanket with my legs out folded
hoping you would meet me with the same warmth I moulded
soft open hands, I would give you the clothes I didn't have spare
I was already vulnerable, laid myself bare
some would call it being a door mat, to love them like your own
but I'd be the first thing you'd see when you arrive into the home
by the door I waited, frame to frame, I lean
I would've taken the muddy prints if it meant that you were clean
it's the only way I know how to love
something I know that I'm worthy of

and if all you did today was rise
so did the sun
and if all you did was stay safe until dark
so did the moon
and if all you did today was sit in the field
so did the flowers
and even if you didn't feel it
today, you still grew

open arms

how much more can you take from me
so many days dissolved in worry
I watched them dissipate before my eyes
I tried to smile
I walked with the anxiety
I even held its hand
I tried to understand its purpose
how did you end up living with me
I walked aimlessly
hoping to tire it
I ended up just carrying it
for I could not watch it suffer
I asked the same for myself
to be carried, once more
as if I had fallen asleep on the sofa
watching cartoons past sunset
I tried to smile, live a good life
what is a good life if not peaceful
what is a good life if not to be carried
sometimes

we all share the same moon
so no matter how different we may be
there is always room
for the light to spread equally

I thought you took my best years
but my best years are any time I am alive
I am breathing — *I can feel the sun*
so how could you take my best years
when the best is still to come

to rebuild

to rebuild is not to find the perfect blocks which fit together
it is about working with what you have left
after your foundation was knocked in stormy weather
sometimes it's just trying your best
its becoming an artist without being taught how to draw
painting using only your fingers
building using nothing at all
just the dust that lingers
it's using the rubble underneath your feet as shelter
to act as a house
until you can build a home

the little things

tomorrow I will learn to love the smell of lavender again
I will make fresh orange juice and feel pulp between my fingers
I will smile at a stranger and tell them I love their hair
I will make pancakes with fresh berries that stain my lips like my first kiss
I will be careful with the insects that land upon me looking for kindness
I will encapsulate the sun and emulate her warmth
tomorrow I will love — love the small things
because if I am lucky enough to receive its promise
I know that the small things will be waiting for me

shedding is a part of growing
the learning, and the not knowing

all I needed

then it was just myself
like it always had been
many came before and many after
the loneliness existed between them
it wrapped itself around my life
dancing with the nostalgia
running with my loved ones
walking with my childhood
but behind that was peace
peace in being alone
then came the strength
because it was just myself
like it always had been
many came before and many after
but I was all that I needed

hold on

I can feel myself slipping
and this journey isn't one
where I can dig my heels into the ground
catch balance
drag my nails through solid rock and dangle until I am saved
it is me diving down cliff edges
painting my body with dirt
it is uncertainty
I know I will resurface, maybe a little bruised
but the colours won't define me
a little more blue inside and out
I know that I will fall again
that's why I have to remain still
be focused, *close my eyes*
hibernate through the cold
I know that strength will carry me
and I can't have strength
if I don't find peace in this

I have lived a great life
I haven't seen much
but I have felt a lot
and I think, as long as I can feel deeply
anywhere is special
everywhere is special

I often wander

I often wonder if I'm living the right life
if I have lived on all sides of the moon
there is so much I want to do
but I am, a pheasant in the road dodging traffic
it's a hard life of feeling
sadness and happiness separated by a hair
split at the ends
but the path leads the same way
the same path I wander
the same path I call
running from fumes
they watch me from the tempered glass
those houses out in the countryside
running on fumes
I found it hard to sleep
I often wonder how it feels to be still
all my life I have been searching for something I cannot find
but I often wander
and follow it in the hopes
that maybe it is searching for me too

I am learning that there is a place for me here
it might be colder, quieter, *lonelier*
than I first imagined
but I will make it my home
I will make it my home

the wedding of dreams

I had a dream last night I got married
on a path that spiralled upwards
a golden sunset graced this city where no one lived
just a lone church on a hill cast in yellow light
I was late to the ceremony
my hair was half done, curled down my back
hanging on a raspberry dress, I've always loved fruit
you stood and looked at me, a half smile
I remember everything about you
it's been six years and my memory is hazy
like the sky we welcomed this day
but you walked me down the aisle and I could feel you
I knew you thought I looked beautiful
your little granddaughter was getting married to the man of her dreams
so far away from teaching me how to swim
I was now learning how to love
grandma was there too
bringing trousers for my uncle who was also late
she always knew how to hold it together
it's like we'd never been apart
the wedding of dreams
the only wedding in my dreams
and I would take it all, just to be together
and that's the thing about imagination
it still happened, even if it was just inside my head

learn to focus

how many hobbies do I have to start
before something reels me in
I'm like a fish out of water
and trying to get my brain to focus
is like trying to put a frayed thread through a needle
and when threaded
it falls out the other side
maybe I'll try knitting but
I'll only finish half the scarf
the other half can wait until winter
I started painting a watercolour cactus
the needles like the ones I thread with
one half scarf
one unfinished painting later
an ambiguous combination
I think tomorrow I might learn the piano

us too, like the trees
show beauty in different tones
in different scenery

the best place to live

your body is your home
so learn to live in it
don't just sleep and eat in it
light candles and incense
dance in the smoke
the forgotten years are remembered
find a patch of sunlight and sit in it
make your bed and plump your pillows
dream in it — *even when you are awake*
invite only the most special guests in
make it a place of love and solitude
don't always tidy up before you see friends
I promise they love you more natural
they see you for who you are inside
comfort, warmth, *a safe space*

fight in the gentleness

what is to fly, *if not to be free*

to the naked eye you were a fragile bird
wings severed to always land on your feet
fleeing from storms although they bring the best fruits
but a naked eye becomes distorted when the glasses are hued with rose
pink streaks on translucent windows
seeing sunsets in charcoal skies
and this fragile bird becomes my morning call
when the nights are too long, too dark
and he becomes
the magpie I saluted with two fingers because he was always alone
a feather on my kitchen table when I didn't cook for two
a hungry jackdaw taking the glasses from my face
you seemed frightened when you saw my naked eyes
did you not recognise me under this moon
it is full like those who love unapologetically
was it an act of instinct or naivety
a rod for your own back, to act as your wings
to reel me in when the summer comes
and cast me into the torrents before the rain brings flowers
but I guess in those moments I felt like I was flying
and that is something I have that you can never take
because what is to fly, *if not to be free*

I want love to caress me gently
touching where you can't see
I know all of its history
now I want it to know me

growth is wanting to make a daisy chain
to wear the flowers like a gown
but realising they do not exist for us
like we do not exist for anybody else

the safety inside

I wonder if we could see inside our bodies
how much more we would love them
the perfect nest inside our stomach
a blanket of warmth, a cocoon of safety
to harbour another part of ourself
and despite the thunder of heartbreak
the crushing feelings of weight when it drops
the butterflies still arrive, when love is present
she tells us when to feel safe, when not to feel safe
and aches for us to listen
she offers us an ear to talk
and carries us — memories from childhood
she holds us, an embrace like a past love
all she asks for is a little kindness
and the least we could do, is give her
what we give to others

I was so desperate to leave the soil
I stood on my own flowers
but I am learning that growth is patience, *forgiveness*
and I'm taking it all in, the seasons and the storms
nurturing what I already have
there is so much time

weaving

love isn't what I thought it would be
its being wrapped around vines and carried with the wind
above the soil where I've been dug out of half alive
brought back to life with only kindness
the same vines that never let me fall off of sharp edges
or when I do, catch me before I lose anymore of myself

I thought love was vanity, which vines grow the tallest
or the prettiest, or have the most visitors
but our vines hold life, they grow in all weathers
and most importantly they are resilient
they withstand the pull of unkind hands
and the feet of many whom are lost

love is the strength of our vine
your hand in mine

in another life

you looked like me but a little kinder
you handed me a four leaf clover
I could see you added an extra leaf on
you told me luck is anywhere that love is
one cannot exist without the other
in another life I am your daughter
but here we exist as two little friends
under the arms of the sun
our feet run through the wet grass
away from the noise and the chaos
I hand you a three leaf clover
and tell you there is beauty in being odd
don't be ashamed to be different
the mud in our feet never mattered, we were growing
luck never existed, our reality was weaved through feeling
like the field we stood upon, raw and organic
kindness was born in our hearts
it grew in the small patches of light
follow it, and never look back

love all of me

I want someone to love all of me
be my light when I wake in the night
be gentle with my anxiety
if you take some of my weight I think I'll be alright

we can be stronger together
I can barely carry myself nowadays
will you love me forever?
I love myself just enough to fight the waves

the winter is always freezing
but its colder out at sea
the door is open for a reason
incase you want to share a tea

I find it hard being alone you see
I'll dance between the kettle steam
pretend the fog has kidnapped me
or maybe it was all a dream

inside my house, safe and warm
all I know is inside this storm

it is all worth it for this

birds stirring in thicket nests
whilst coffee is stirred with a silver spoon
and the silver moon smiles to the sun
an alluring sight to see dividing light
summon one another
no jealously just acceptance of their differences
and the call of the birds whistling in the blossom haze
with each weaving note forming the perfect melody
fusing like the foliage in their homes
enough to calm the coastline
and pull the tides back from the moon

starting again

this is what it's like to feel the rain
the burden of wet clothes
as they force you to the floor like gravity's hold
I think I've felt this before and now I can't go outside
and I've been trying to find my home
you don't know strength until you carry everything you've ever owned
lost in the clear dust
I only needed to stay straight
empathetic, kind, a good heart
but it was the overtaking
the trailing behind
mud collecting like old antiques
no value in this road
I let go of everything I knew
tossed my belongings for the foxes to find
don't ever fear the naked lady sitting beneath the pine and oak
she is being born again
the rain felt less heavy
the sun was always light
nothing was constant but everything stayed
the weight of the world was easier to hold

night is calling but we are just rising

to love like the moon

we don't need to leave this here
we can be as one
we can love each other
like the moon loves the sun
we can live like them
up in the sky
where it's just us
nothing passes us by
maybe a few birds
maybe a few planes
i'll give you the light
if you give me the rain
in the depths of this harsh weather
it's easier when we're shining together

the light that keeps on giving

look how much you've grown
despite the crashing waves
where the birds haven't flown
not even for days
found a way to stand tall
a timeless oak tree
you have blossomed through it all
even on days you don't see
strangers come to visit you at sunset
lovers kissing under your leaves
alone, but together as a silhouette
they feel safe in your company
you help love to flourish
despite not seeing it in you
it takes so much courage
to give light, *when you need it too*

a gentle life

what is more gentle
than a heart that hasn't been touched
or a heart touched so deeply
that it can never give up
a small bird I carry back to health
these hands that hold love as wealth
he nests on my branches
with me he takes his chances
no handprint is the same
and all my lines are arranged
a path to simplicity
I follow in sympathy
I can leave tonight
a gentle life is travelling light

it was saying nothing that said so much
the silence left room for us to exist together

letting go of myself

I missed her as I washed my clothes
I thought about her as I drank my coffee
I touched her in my dreams
I cried for her over breakfast
she touched me in my nightmares
we danced at sunset
where nobody could see us
in the shadows of each other
I let her go at sunrise
I must not let her back in
I wondered if she was cold outside
I hugged her — one last time

stripped bare

I've had the same bed for ten years
and I know I should get a new one
but it feels like I'm breaking up with a partner
love dampened by midnight rain
or ending a friendship
you know has run it's course
yet you still try and keep up with the pace
this bed has carried me
pillars weak from years of adventures
slanted posts from gifted pressure
you provided a space
to weave bodies
to steal bodies
but I forgive you
many times I wasn't there
I didn't always return home to you
but you forgave me
a relationship in which we've both been stripped bare
to make eachother up again
and remind us how we should be loved

I need to remember that
if I don't know whether to sink or swim
I can just float
it is ok to be still
it is ok to let the waves console me
it is ok to make the water my home
it is ok to let it take some weight
to let it cleanse me
to let it feel me
to let it teach me
and only then can I swim

a story in a story

another day in our rich tapestry of life
I hung it on my wall to remind me
the art in simplicity
threaded cotton clouds
raining material to be used as shelter
woven insects
each one with an important job to fulfil
the birds nestle in the elements
whilst they hunger for the worms
and the trees talk through energy
ancient embroidered roots
each ring symbolising another year
the circle of this rich life
cast across my bedroom
stories within stories

it's a bittersweet notion — moving on
I am letting go of so much
but I am gaining *so much more*

where it all started

I sat in my room at seven years old
when monsters climbed out from under the beds of children
and wondered how life never stopped
it just kept going
and even at seven I was so aware of my existence
I knew that if there were monsters under my bed
that they would be my friends
because empathy sat on my bedside table
I didn't want anyone to not feel wanted
not even monsters
I wasn't afraid of the dark but I was afraid of eternal darkness
and leaving my family, and even at seven
I knew that life would be so different for someone like me

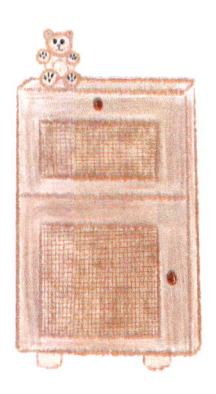

I closed my eyes
    tight enough that I began to imagine
        my flowers blooming
            but not too tight
        that I missed myself
                grow

I started to heal inside
the more time I spent outside
time stopped and everything felt important
but nothing truly mattered

the fruits of our labour

I carry nostalgia with me
it comes in waves, avocado coloured ripples
it pulls me like the moon pulls the tides
a feeling of longing
wavering grief
even though this chapter of my life is the fullest
I sometimes struggle to stay afloat
the feeling I felt watching normal people for the first time
or songs that remind me of summer 16
the smell of my first sweet vanilla perfume
passing places I used to go
does the water want to keep me young
I must grow up one day
twenty six is dawning and she is a mango coloured sun
subtle saffron skies
I'm hoping she will calm the waves
and carry me to my thirties with ease

art form

I want to make so much art
I sit amongst grass hills
where I birthed each flower
I want to be known for my creativity
my whole life a painting
I want to be a mum
to create little versions of me
I want to be kind
to create a space for empathy
I want to be generous
create extra pieces of myself to gift people
I want to be happy
the first thing you see when you look at me
a beam of light
like the heavens have opened
I don't want to hear she is beautiful
I want to hear
she is art

love must exist
a good love
a pure love
a simple love
a "let's work this out together" love
a "I have listened to your favourite album" love
a "we are rich because we are happy" love
because that is the way I love
and I need to remember that if I feel it
it must also exist outside my heart

sureness in the uncertainty

twenty something

I caught the plague we all seem to get in our twenties
I heard it's passed between sensitive souls on winter nights
it crawled under my skin when I needed warmth
and I found it hard to let it go
uncertainty disguised as yearning
can I be kinder
is this where I belong
am I happy
twenty five, wanting all the answers
under the third quarter moon
in this first quarter of my life
time is passing anyway, even if I try to fight it
I needed the sun on my bones
so I waited for her arrival
the first time I could breathe
time is passing slower
the warmth is moving closer
this is where I belong

I hope I'm going to be someone great
I'm just not sure how long that'll take
be patient my hearts says
just make it through the day

you are home

keep pushing through uncomfortable rooms
keep walking into them even if you're alone
even if they're busy and full of people you don't know
keep walking into these rooms like you own the floor
you never know which ones you're going to light up
some will already have candles
some will already have fairy lights
some will be busy
some will be quiet
but there will be rooms you walk into
dark and desolate
you will light up the floor
bring conversation to strangers lips
some of them waiting for your exact glow
and it will start to feel like home
then before you even know it
you will bring home
to every room you're in

maybe just existing is enough
maybe being me, *is the best thing I'll ever be*

complacent

why did I stay where I was comfy
I love comfort
but it does have a habit
of keeping you contained
if it's cold outside
you don't want to move out the warm
but it is the cold
that makes you feel alive

you can't hide from growth
it is happening all around us

so
much
to
lose

so
much
to
gain

who am i
to pick
between
the heart
and
the brain

leading with love

I wonder if I will ever be loved in the way that I need
I don't think they understand my brain
I don't think they understand my heart
to lead with love is bittersweet
it runs in front, but I always catch it
I hold its hand and we skip amongst the daises
I live for little moments, don't think ahead too much
but I am met with responsibility
and you can't run with responsibility, you see
it doesn't like to feel free like love does
I think it wants me to be sensible
practical, *forward thinking*
but it is hard
I can't be something I am not
we can get through anything with love
what is more important than that?

my sheep

I watched him pluck his eyebrows
at midnight in the bathroom, with the small light on
he never let me do it
maybe it was a sign
he didn't trust me to be gentle
although I carried his heart for five years
I never dropped it once, I never lost it
but I think I carried it deeper than he'd have liked to venture
I knew tomorrow he would be gone
I knew he was going far - to take his heart away
why is it only okay when he does it?
I couldn't raise my voice
but he could erupt like a heated volcano
I only wanted to do his eyebrows
make him look nice
he said my toothbrush was never charged
but he never needed to charge his
in hindsight I think he was using mine for fun
who am I going to draw pictures in the clouds with now?
that big cotton bird you always said looked like a sheep
I thought it did too, but it was only okay when you said it
maybe I'll be alone when the sun pours honey into the sky
a yellow mirage
and my tea has gone cold from thinking for too long
but at least when the moon births sheep for me to count
they will be my sheep and not his

handle with care

he told me I wasn't good at handling my emotions
although my hands were soft
I was kind and compassionate
I knew exactly how to be gentle
but with each grey day I clenched my jaw
too much pressure
and each blue day I let myself go
not enough support
then I handled them in my winter gloves
I couldn't feel anything
but the December night frost
everytime I became overwhelmed
I handed them on, like they were recycled clothes
I wanted them to walk in my shoes
to know how it feels to be different
I juggled them for entertainment
dropping parts of me, in places I passed
all I needed to do was hold them
when they called for me
like a newborn needing milk
and put them down
once the moon shone through
a time for peace
play white noise
sleep next to them
only handle them
when they need me

the luck of seven

I started to feel like I wasn't good enough
seven days I wondered why I hadn't smiled
each glimpse in the mirror gave me seven years of bad luck
I tucked my head between my arms
on the sofa, underneath the blanket
it's too cold to open my eyes
I wasn't sleeping to recharge my brain
I was sleeping to stop my brain
from crafting thoughts
seven penetrated my skin
like the bed of roses I imagined myself in
each one told me I wouldn't make it here
below the window I slept, the planes left trails
above my head, *for me to follow*
three hundred people sat in that plane
they couldn't see me but I could see them
a little metal basket gliding through the blue
suddenly I was not so small
seven billion people share a rock
seven thoughts were too many

rebirth

this is the first day of my life
today I am reborn
I have reclaimed all my innocence
my naivity summons me
the need for comfort
although I am cold
screaming for attention
I am safe
I can't support my head but
I never could anyway
my eyes open just enough
to soak in the tears of joy
for my existence
I cry on my mothers chest and she holds me
not much has changed
still finding comfort in white noise
the womb a distinct memory
but I am here
I am born
and my existence alone
has moved a room full of people
like the april tides
on the month of my birth
constant and fierce

we didn't know if there would be rain or sun
but we had love
and that was enough to make the day last

the unity of loneliness

anxiety is a blanket term that covers so many of us
but isn't it comforting to know that when underneath it
at least we can share each others warmth

I couldn't tell the sky from the sea
but still — I'm jumping in
letting it take all of me

it is who we are

I'm starting to think
what I will truly remember
when the time comes
what I will hold in my hands
will it be how my hair sat perfectly on my shoulder
like blades of grass moving effortlessly in the wind
or how my stomach was flat enough to balance a sand timer
for me to lose myself in how long I spent looking in the mirror
how good I was at counting *calories*
or will it be how comfortable the birds felt around me
how I was soft and gentle
how I could calm a roaring fire
how my body aligned with the sun and the moon
how many connections I made
how many souls I touched
how many flowers I grew
even if they have now wilted
if I never grew them
I wouldn't know true beauty
they say it's better to have loved and lost
but what about to live
and hold onto that, *forever*

life will tell you to wake before the sun and
chase your dreams, but living gently means
rising with her and letting your dreams find
you — *patience, my love*

beyond the blue

I don't want to die because I feel like I haven't lived yet
but I've spent everyday living, afraid of dying
the irony sits comfy in the middle
between the paradoxical waves
I watch them crash against the window
awaiting the day I can dip my feet into gentle water
and not anticipate it washing me away

a moment in time

I love the woman I am becoming
younger me would be beaming
from one little ear to the other
like the sun hugging the skies
in my arms she would be
I would tell her not to fear
your kind heart will serve you
your love of animals will build you
your sensitivity will enlighten you
in the mirage of the rays
a summer morning in '09
school is nearly starting
and the grass has just been cut
she is running to me
and I am waiting to catch her

they will miss your soul

it is almost as if I can hear it
a call beckoning me from the unknown
I must live like I have been given a second chance at this life
like I knelt before him and bargained
promises of simplicity
to stand with those who live in the shadows
echos turn into bird calls
I have so much that needs to be said
to see my family again
so many lost words
at night you can hear them
often in the big trees
there will be tears
so many tears
but in the midst of the waves
forgotten worries
they don't miss my appearance
they don't think of my weight
the style of my hair or makeup
it is my soul they need
to leave peace to make peace
to remember what's important

they have waited patiently for the rain
and *so have I*

love and compromise

they said this was learning
this was growing
this is what it should feel like to love
it hurts and it's complicated
but it is simple and kind
is this what it should feel like
to live for two people instead of one
or should we find a way to live in each other's hands
where we don't want to put each other down
but sometimes we have too
the most gentle touch
they say love is compromise
taking the bad times with the good
and love shouldn't feel like this
but sometimes it should

I'm not going to be scared
to look at the scales anymore
because with all the extra love I have
and with all the extra happiness I've gained
no wonder I am heavier

someday

I want to believe in reincarnation
so I can come back as all the versions of myself
the ones I missed in this lifetime
somewhere, maybe someday
it is Sunday and I don't have to get up for work
I live in a little Volkswagen van off grid
this is where I learn to draw
then maybe it is Monday and I am learning piano
I sing the night we met by Lord Huron
so beautifully
that the birds flock to my stain glass window
it is here that I dance
I am greeted by the moon
then his sister, the sun
she is shy but tender
it is a summer morning in July
my window overlooks acres of land
cows, sheep and grass overgrown
it is here that I reminisce
then it is today and I am writing this poem
my fingers can't type fast enough for the excitement of life
I am worried I will not experience all that I can be
it is here that I will try

to sail the waves, is to ride the storms
we aren't always prepared
but we always find a way to stay warm

a lot more to love

I promised myself I wouldn't mourn the body of my teenage years
yearning for something that hadn't even developed
that wasn't healthy
that hadn't even been loved yet
I look at it and see the beauty in being skinny
but forget to see the sadness that came with it
now I am loved
I am ready to hold another life inside me
to grow and nurture something with nothing but myself
I am heavier because I took the time to have breakfast with loved ones
cups of coffee in crowded corners
probably too much sugar but that never mattered
I shared late night takeaways with my best friend
where we talked about everything over pizza
there is nothing better to confide in
I saw the value in memories over food
and it helped make them more special
I miss myself sometimes but I don't need her anymore
I need a body that will support me
and I will promise to love all of it in return
especially now that there is a lot more to love

slow down

I've spent the last few years trying to see the good in feeling too much
I've felt the depths of the ocean without even swimming in it
they say only ten percent of it has been explored but I know it all
each wave has kissed my skin
I know each animal by name
I have lived each season before it's come around
every month has felt like a year
but I finally feel like I'm living
my greatest memories just sitting under a tree
because each flower has a different story
the big moments are too overwhelming
I need time to feel everything properly
that's often why I need quiet
simplicity
because if there is too much to feel
I will feel it all at once
but if there isn't a lot to feel
I can get to know it — *slowly*

and on the day the sun set for the last time in my mind
all I could think of was a tender may morning
birds calling to the beat of my heart
the quiet things
and oh, I would go back and stay in those moments longer
before I become part of the Earth
before I become those moments
teaching the same lessons, *that I wish I knew sooner*

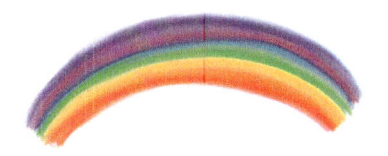

the end

goodbye, for now

if you have made it until the end, thank you from the bottom of my heart. This was never intended to be a self help book, just an exploration into the deepest parts of my soul, the struggles, the pain, the confusion, the beauty and the reflection. I used to be embarrassed to feel, and would write poems and keep them hidden inside a notebook, oh, what a waste. I realised that feeling deeply unlocked some of the most beautiful moments in my life, and even in the darkest times, there was always a little patch of sunlight if I looked hard enough. Now I know that I must follow this light, and wherever it will guide me, is where I need to be. The same goes for you, my love, keep going, *enjoy the ride,* and never stop feeling.

Printed in Great Britain
by Amazon